Storage

Leather

Water

barometer

…ly 9 Cannon

S S S S

Twelve hundred fiery serpents…

Cylinder

clay, sand hay, straw

SOMETIMES

THE MOON COMES NEAR THE EARTH AND OTHER TIMES IT MOVES AWAY FROM IT

- Map (Mappa selenographica) thermometer

compass lorgnette

- 2 dogs
- Clothes for every season - Blankets
- Tools (hammers, saw)
- Boxes / seeds
- seeds soil trees
- Cans of food (meat + vegetables)
- water for 2 months

In the same series
AROUND THE WORLD IN 80 DAYS
20,000 LEAGUES UNDER THE SEA
JOURNEY TO THE CENTRE OF THE EARTH
FROM THE EARTH TO THE MOON

From the Earth to the Moon

Published in hardback in Great Britain in 2019 by
Faros Books Limited, Turret House, Station Road, Amersham, Buckinghamshire, HP7 0AB

ISBN 978-1-9164091-5-6

Text © 2018 Antonis Papatheodoulou
Illustrations © 2018 Iris Samartzi
Translation by Maria Mountokalaki
The right of Antonis Papatheodoulou and Iris Samartzi to be identified as
the author and illustrator of this work has been asserted by them
in accordance with the Copyright, Designs and Patents Act, 1988

A catalogue record for this book is available from the British Library

Printed in Greece
Visit our website at www.farosbooks.co.uk

From the Earth to the Moon or A Cannon for Peace

Retold by
ANTONIS
PAPATHEODOULOU

Illustrated by
IRIS
SAMARTZI

FarosBooks

It is 1865, on a full moon night, and we find ourselves on the porch of a beautiful house in Baltimore, U.S.A. The house belongs to Impey Barbicane, the country's most famous weapons designer.

But what exactly is he doing sitting on his porch? He usually stays at work till late, designing ever-more powerful weapons, and cannons that can shoot even further. Why isn't he there now?

It's because the war is over. People set aside their differences and remembered the things they had in common. Battlefields were turned back into fields; army headquarters were transformed again into farmhouses; the soldiers returned home. And so did Impey Barbicane.

Sitting in his rocking chair, on his porch, he finally had some time to think.

Ahh, peacetime is nice, he thought, looking up at the moon. *Only now there is no need for armourers anymore. To be honest, building cannons to demolish houses and fortresses and sink ships with, is not the best way to make a living. But I do my job very well,* he reflected, still gazing at the moon. *If only there were peaceful cannons. I'd build them better than anyone . . .*

"That's it!"

he cried out after a second.

The moon had given him a great idea. "The world's greatest cannon would enrich humankind with new knowledge; it would fire cannonballs not at enemies, but all the way to the surface of the unexplored moon. Yes! That would be a cannon for peace."

And so, Impey Barbicane fell asleep in his rocking chair, dreaming of peaceful cannons and of journeys to the moon.

Very early the following morning he set off to visit the Observatory at Cambridge in Massachusetts. With his nose deep in books, he pored over maps and diagrams, and put questions to the most famous astronomy professors. He wanted to learn everything there was to know about the moon. Here is what he found out:

- The moon is almost a quarter the size of the earth.
- A lunar day lasts about as long as 30 days on earth.
- A part of the moon is invisible from earth and no one knows what secrets it holds.
- The moon's orbit is elliptical, so that sometimes it draws closer to the earth and other times it moves away from it.
- The cannonball would have to travel for four whole days to reach the moon.
- In order for the cannonball to reach the moon, it would have to be launched at a speed of 40,000 kilometers per hour.
- On the fourth of December the following year, the moon would come very close to the Earth – a rare opportunity for him to try his experiment, since it wouldn't approach so much again for eighteen years!

The very next day, Impey Barbicane announced his idea to other armourers around the country. The news spread across the United States and all over the world. Newspapers and magazines dedicated whole articles to the crazy idea of a cannon whose projectile could reach the moon not to wage war, but to offer newfound knowledge to humankind.

Thousands of good-luck letters and offers of help flooded into Impey Barbicane's office. Armourers, astronomers, scientists, politicians, journalists, and military people, young and old, all were enthusiastic about his idea.

All but one, that is: Captain Nicholl, builder of cannonball-resistant naval ships, who was not very fond of armourers. He didn't believe their plan would succeed.

It's impossible! You will never make it! Your plan will fail. I am willing to bet on that.

Impey Barbicane had no time to lose. He formed a team of the finest armourers and called J. T. Maston, the most experienced cannon designer, to his aid. First they had to draw up plans for a large projectile and then design a cannon big enough for it to fit in.

There were endless problems to be dealt with.

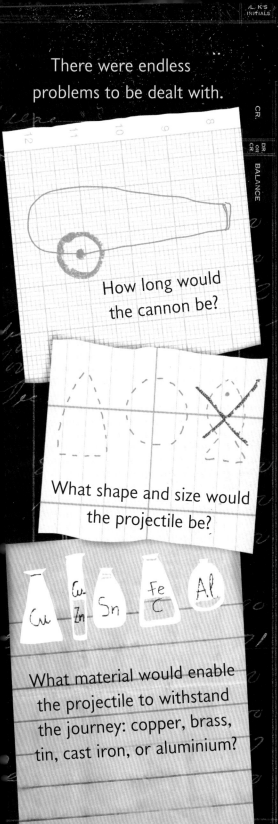

How long would the cannon be?

What shape and size would the projectile be?

What material would enable the projectile to withstand the journey: copper, brass, tin, cast iron, or aluminium?

Impey Barbicane and J. T. Maston wrote and rewrote feverishly, drawing up plans and doing calculations on big rolls of paper. Major Elphinstone, the team's chemist, conducted experiments to determine the type of gunpowder most suitable for the blast inside the huge cannon.

But then, Impey Barbicane began receiving contributions from all corners of the world. Scientists and laypeople from every country put in as much money as they could afford. Contributions to the great experiment flooded in: everybody wants to help out towards a peaceful goal.

The designs were ready but there was still one problem they had to solve. Where would they find the money to build the cannon? Their astronomical experiment was astronomically expensive!

Everybody, that is, except Captain Nicholl who didn't send money; he sent letters:

"It is impossible to build such an enormous cannon!
Such a huge cannonball cannot be shot!
Your cannon will implode!
The iron will melt!
This plan is destined to fail, and I am willing to bet on it," he insisted.

Indeed, it wasn't easy. Once they got to the launching ground in Tampa, Florida, they had to overcome one obstacle after another.

The cannon had to be 270 metres tall! How on earth would they ever prop it up?

After some thought, they decided to build the cannon underground! They would dig a deep well and pour metal into it.

TAMPA

STONE'S HILL

Also they needed tons of iron and hundreds of furnaces to melt this metal and workers who would spend months constructing it.

But Impey Barbicane and his partners were determined. They had the iron imported by ship and even constructed a railway to transport the metal to them.

Then they built a whole town in Tampa where the 1,500 workers and their families would live while the cannon was being built.

After eight months of hard work, the well was ready. Molten iron was poured into it and everyone waited for it to take the shape of the gigantic cannon. The heat was infernal and the ground was sweltering hot; you couldn't walk around Tampa anymore.

As soon as the cannon was completed, visitors started flooding in. They travelled down the well in baskets to marvel at it. Toasts were made by Impey Barbicane and his partners inside the massive cannon. 270 metres below the surface of the earth, they opened a bottle of wine and clinked their glasses: "Here's to the moon!" they cheered in unison.

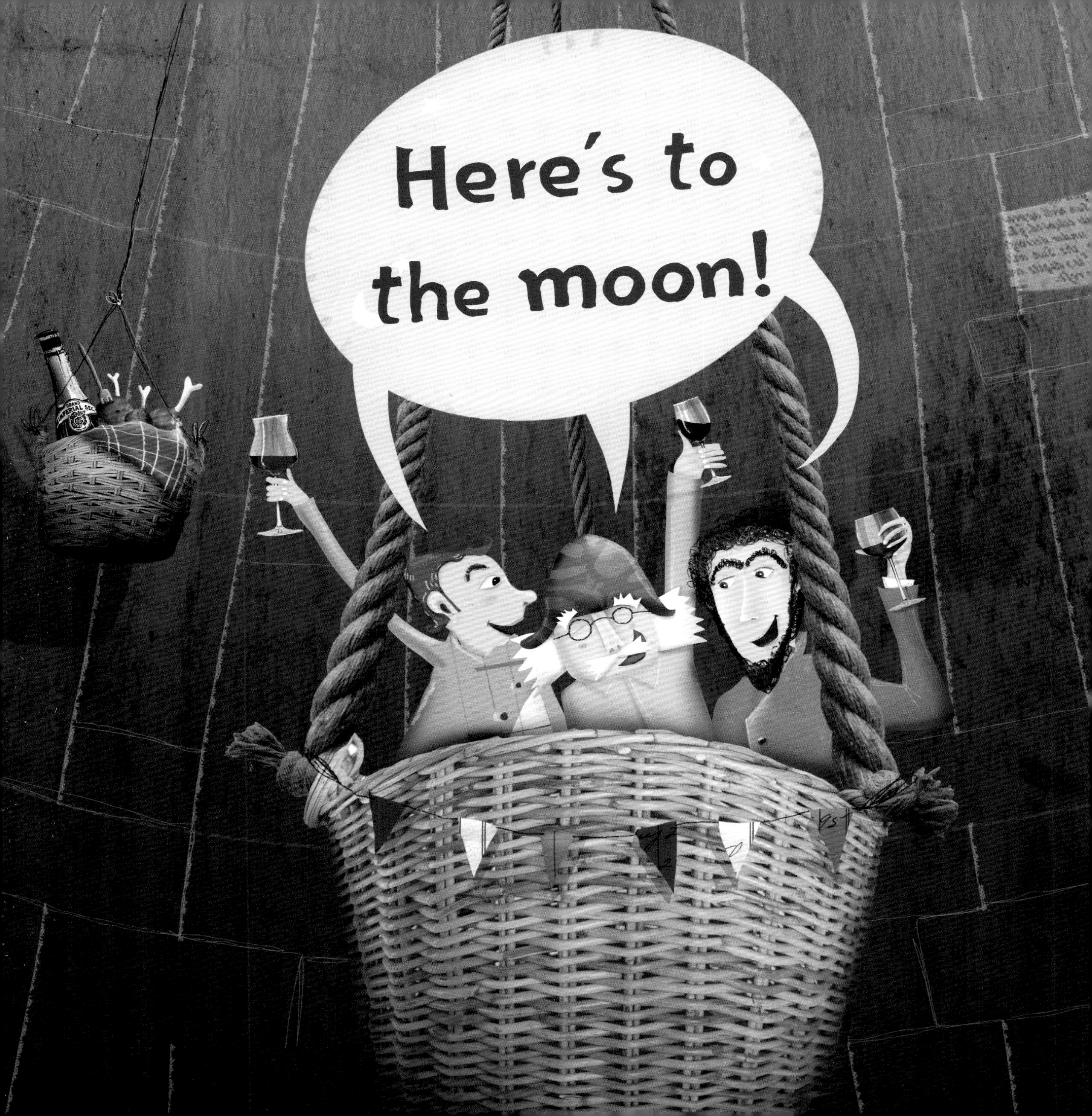
Here's to the moon!

The armourers were now ready to construct the cannonball. But a letter arrived
that was to alter their plans completely:

To: Impey Barbicane
        Gentlemen!
Do not make a round cannonball.
Make it cylindro-conical instead.
    And hollow. I would
        like to go inside it
    and travel to the moon.
    I am arriving by steamer.

                    Signed, Michel Ardan

This was beyond the armourers' wildest dreams. A courageous Frenchman, Michel Ardan, wanted to get inside the projectile! This would no longer be a mere experiment. It would be a real journey. The first journey to the moon.

Impey Barbicane thought it was all a hoax. But he was wrong. Michel Ardan did come to Tampa and delivered a moving speech to the thousands of people who had gathered to welcome him.

It takes courage to move forward!
Consider this. First humans walked on all fours and then we stood
up on our own two feet; we rode horses, then wagons, then trains
and now it's time to go even further: to travel to the moon
in a projectile! Mark my words! It will not be
just me travelling to the moon. Humanity itself will gain
knowledge from this journey. We shall all reach the moon.
Together!

"I'll come," Impey Barbicane offered.
"I'll join you inside the projectile."
"Me too," added another voice.
It was Captain Nicholl! Even he had been convinced
for the greatness of the coming journey. The cannon
of peace had already had its first victory.

The projectile was built like a small house for the three of them. It had an entrance, windows, and all the essential supplies: air to breathe, water to drink, food to eat, light and heavy clothing, tools, scientific instruments, and maps of the moon. J. T. Maston himself offered to stay in the projectile for a few days to test it, before his three courageous friends set off.

Michel Ardan got carried away with excitement. "We should take horses with us, so we have transportation; and donkeys, so they can carry our supplies; and cows, so we have plenty of milk."

Luckily, Impey Barbicane was more sensible. "Our projectile is a scientific craft, my dear Ardan, not Noah's Ark!"

On the night of December the first, thousands of people gathered in Tampa to watch the launch.

Even the moon had drawn closer to the earth as if it, too, wanted to admire the three brave explorers. What a touching farewell. What a great day for humankind!

The engineers got ready.

3 2 1

FiRe!

The blast was deafening! The enormous cannon erupted like a volcano and sent the projectile flying into the atmosphere, filling Tampa's sky with flames. The ground began to shake as though a huge earthquake had occurred, and everything was covered in smoke!

For days afterwards, J. T. Maston observed the moon through the big telescope at the Observatory, trying to locate the projectile. He could only peer through it with a single eye, but it was as if the eyes of the whole world were looking together.

Then, on December the twelfth, a tiny speckle appeared to be revolving around the moon. It was the projectile! And if the telescope had been able to zoom in even more, J. T. Maston would have been able to see the faces of his three friends, full of amazement and curiosity, observing the earth's satellite from up close.

Impey Barbicane's cannon for peace had made it, and for the three adventurers the journey around the moon had begun.

Antonis Papatheodoulou was born in Athens. He has published more than 50 books for children, some of which have been translated into eleven languages. They have also been adapted into plays and for puppet theatre, and have won many awards, including two Greek State Picture Book Awards and the 2016 International Compostela Prize. Five of his books have been included in the White Ravens list of the International Children's Library of Munich. Discover more about Antonis and his work at www.antonispapatheodoulou.com.

Iris Samartzi is a children's book illustrator and an art teacher. Her work has received many awards, including the 2016 International Compostela Prize for Picture Books, the Greek State Picture Book Award (2012, 2016) and the Greek IBBY Award (2012, 2015, 2016 and 2017). When she is not illustrating books, she runs art workshops for children. She lives and works in Athens, Greece. Read more about Iris and her work at www.irissamartzi.com.